TO ISABELLE -

I HOPE YOU ENJOY THE JOURNEY!

BEST WISHES,

Debbie Butter

TONGA

• THE AFRICAN ELEPHANT STORY •

WRITTEN BY: **DEBBIE BUTTAR**   ILLUSTRATED BY: **CHRISTOPHER DAVIS**

GMEC PUBLISHING
LAKE TAHOE, NV

Published by GMEC Publishing
P.O. Box 4470
Lake Tahoe, NV 89449-4470

Publisher's Cataloging-in-Publication Data
Buttar, Debbie.

Tonga the African elephant story / Debbie Buttar; illustrated by Christopher Davis. – Lake Tahoe, NV : GMEC Pub., 2008.

p. ; cm.
Summary: Three African elephants go on a journey to see African animals. In reality, they live in a protected elephant sanctuary in Tennessee.

ISBN: 978-0-9794302-0-6

1. African elephant—Fiction. 2. Elephants—Fiction. I. Davis, Christopher, ill. II. Title.

PZ10.3.B88 To 2008
808.8/99282—dc22   2007932222

Project coordination by Jenkins Group, Inc • www.BookPublishing.com

Printed in Singapore
12 11 10 09 08 • 5 4 3 2 1

The sun was rising, a new day was beginning...

Tonga, Zahara & Kora were just waking from a full nights sleep.

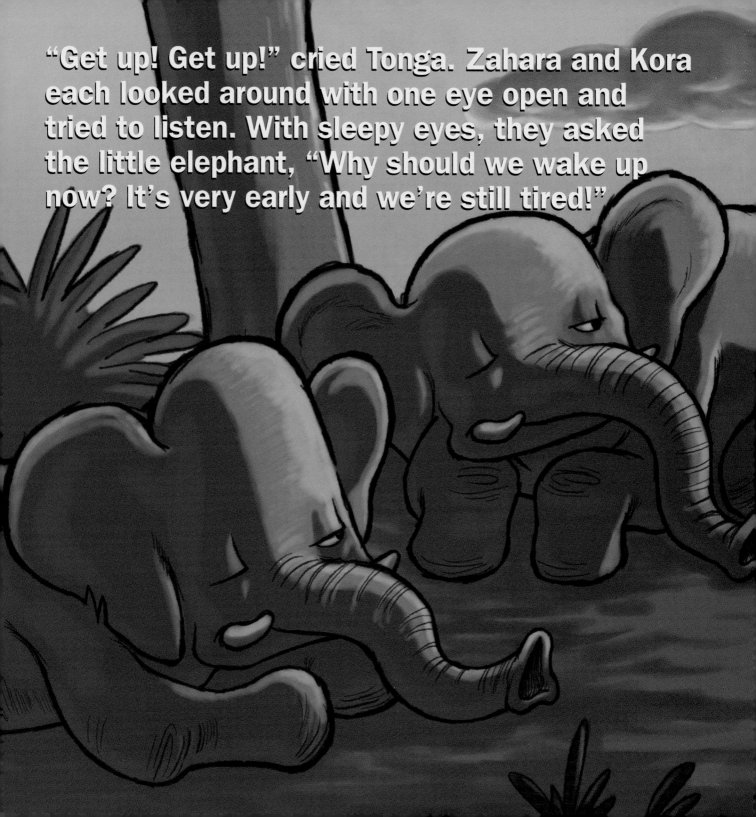

"Get up! Get up!" cried Tonga. Zahara and Kora each looked around with one eye open and tried to listen. With sleepy eyes, they asked the little elephant, "Why should we wake up now? It's very early and we're still tired!"

"Today we're going to explore the open plains of Africa," said Tonga. "I want to see zebras, hyenas, lions, impalas, and hippos. I am so excited! Let's go now!" she trumpeted.

Tonga took off toward the open field. Zahara and Kora sluggishly got up and followed Tonga on her journey. Ba-boom, boom, boom went the rumble of their feet. Ba-boom, boom, boom.

"Look, look!" Tonga shouted. A flash of black and white darted across the field. "Is that a Zebra running across the plain?"

Zahara and Kora looked. "No, that's just a black and white horse," said Kora. "That's what you see. Let's continue our journey." Tonga, Zahara and Kora thundered on. Ba-boom, boom, boom.

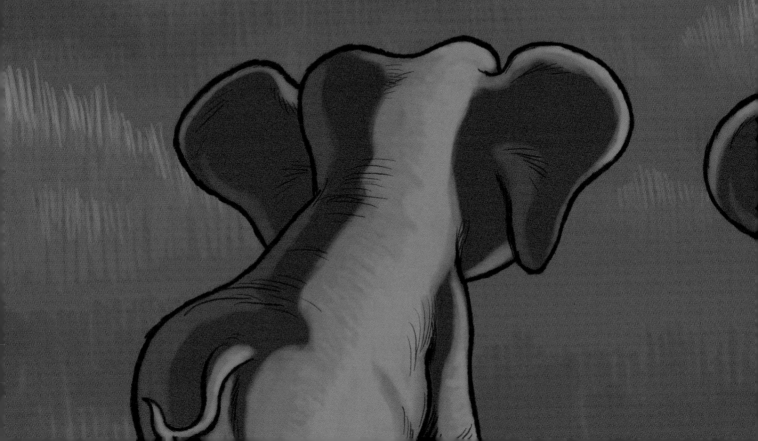

Tonga's eyes grew wider as she saw something hiding behind the tree. "Look, look!" she cried.

"Is that a hyena hiding behind the tree?"

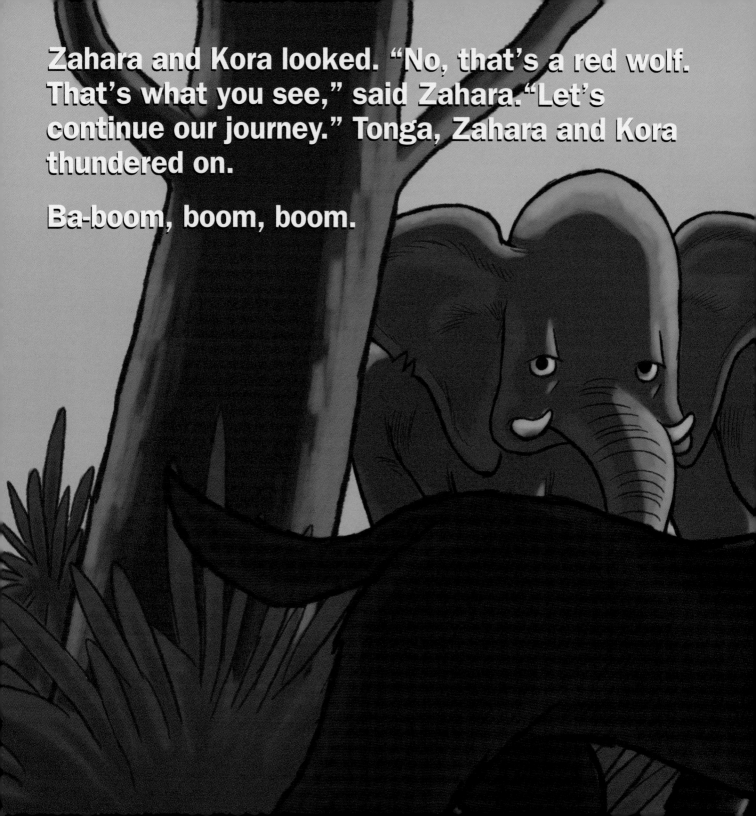

Zahara and Kora looked. "No, that's a red wolf. That's what you see," said Zahara. "Let's continue our journey." Tonga, Zahara and Kora thundered on.

Ba-boom, boom, boom.

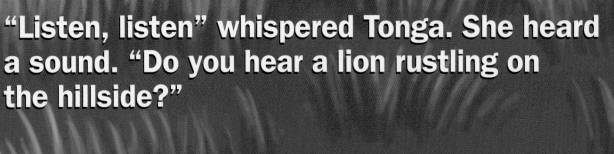

"Listen, listen" whispered Tonga. She heard a sound. "Do you hear a lion rustling on the hillside?"

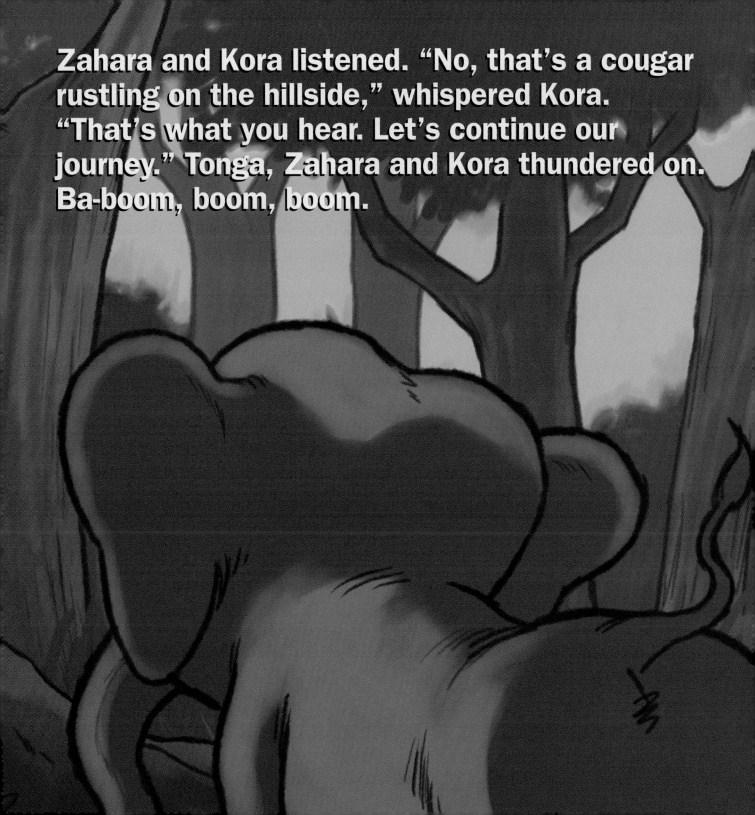

Zahara and Kora listened. "No, that's a cougar rustling on the hillside," whispered Kora. "That's what you hear. Let's continue our journey." Tonga, Zahara and Kora thundered on. Ba-boom, boom, boom.

Tonga, Zahara and Kora kept walking. They came upon a pond, so they stopped for a fresh drink. "Look, look!" cried Tonga. "Do you see an impala taking a drink at the edge of the pond?"

Zahara and Kora looked. "No, that's a white-tailed-deer," said Zahara. "That's what you see at the edge of the pond." Tonga, Zahara and Kora thundered on. Ba-boom, boom, boom.

"Listen, listen!" Tonga said.
"Do you hear a hippo splashing in the water?"

Zahara and Kora listened carefully and looked toward the pond. Kora said "I see a black bear searching for fish. That's what you hear in the pond."

Tonga was so confused. She didn't see a zebra, a hyena, a lion, an impala or a hippo as she thought she should see in Africa. "Zahara and Kora," she said, "why did we see a black and white horse, a red wolf, a cougar, a white-tailed deer, and a black bear today? How could that be if we're living in Africa?"

"Listen Tonga, we are African elephants but we don't live in Africa," explained Kora. "We live in Tennessee!"

"We live in a special place for elephants," said Zahara. "We live in the wild but we are protected. That's why we didn't see all of those African animals."

Tonga smiled. "Well, it feels like home to me," she said. "I wouldn't want to be anywhere else in the world!"

For Rahan, Alexa, Abie, Harry, and
Sara. Sweet Dreams—D.B.

For my Mother and all her support.
—C.D.

GMEC Publishing

P.O. Box 4470

Lake Tahoe, NV 89449-4470